Grandma Drove the Lobsterboat

Written by
Katie Clark

Illustrated by
Amy Huntington

ISBN 978-1-60893-004-3

Library of Congress
Cataloging-in-Publication Data
available on request

Design by Rich Eastman

Printed in Yuanzhou, China August 2016

Down East Books
www.nbnbooks.com
Distributed by
National Book Network
800-462-6420

To Ellie and Daniel

— K.C.

To Captain Jake

— A.H.

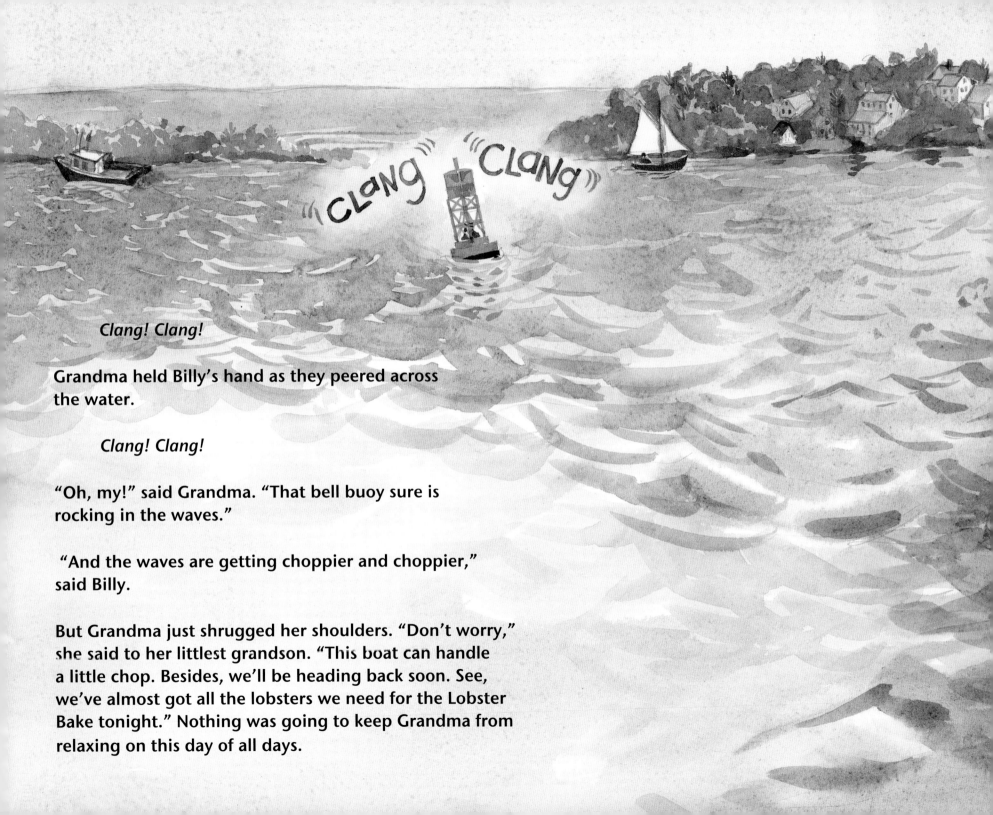

Clang! Clang!

Grandma held Billy's hand as they peered across
the water.

Clang! Clang!

"Oh, my!" said Grandma. "That bell buoy sure is
rocking in the waves."

"And the waves are getting choppier and choppier,"
said Billy.

But Grandma just shrugged her shoulders. "Don't worry,"
she said to her littlest grandson. "This boat can handle
a little chop. Besides, we'll be heading back soon. See,
we've almost got all the lobsters we need for the Lobster
Bake tonight." Nothing was going to keep Grandma from
relaxing on this day of all days.

Every other day of the summer Grandma was busy running the garbage business, while her three sons drove the trucks. And all winter long she was busy running the office for the snowplowing business, too. But today was Labor Day—and Grandma had the day off.

Everyone in town looked forward to the Labor Day Lobster Bake almost as much as Grandma did. Roy Hardy always brought the corn. Edna Fillmore baked dozens of pies. Little Maggie Wells and her family dug bushels of clams. And Grandma's sons provided the lobsters. On this one day of the year, all Grandma had to do was settle back and enjoy the ride.

Whauughh. Whauughh.

Grandma sat down and unscrewed the top to her thermos.

Whauughh. Whauughh.

"Oh, heavens!" said Grandma. "That fog horn sure does go off in the teeny-weeniest bit of fog."

"And the fog is getting thicker and thicker," said Billy.

But Grandma just took a long sip of coffee. "Don't worry," she said. "A little fog won't hurt anybody. Besides, it's got to be time to head back. We're full up with lobsters." She stretched out her legs and took a deep breath of sea air.

Aaghh. . .Aaghh. . .

Grandma glanced toward the stern of the boat.

"Oh, no!" said Grandma. "That youngest son of mine
sure does get seasick with the slightest tip of the boat."

Aaghh. . .Aaghh. . .

"And his knees are getting wobblier and wobblier," said Billy.

Now, Grandma wanted to say, "don't worry" again. But one more look
at Bill and she knew Little Billy was right. Bill could hardly stand up.
There was no way he was going to bring the boat around, much less
steer it back to shore.

"Let's call Buster," said Grandma. "He's just to the east of us. Surely it'll
be no bother for him to swing by and help us home."

But when Billy dialed there was no answer.
Buster was having a terrible time of his own.

"Then we'll get hold of Burt," said Grandma. "He's just to the west of us. Surely it'll be no problem for him to come and help us out."

But when Billy tried the radio there was only static.

Burt was no better off than Buster.

"Drat!" said Grandma. "Double drat! A boat-load of lobsters and no captain to get them to the best party of the season." She kicked the bait bucket. Billy kicked the bait bucket, too.

Then, at the very same time, they both looked up and their frowns turned into smiles.

"Are you thinking what I'm thinking?" said Grandma.

"Sure am," said Billy. "After all, you drove
a garbage truck and a snowplow, right?"

"Then what are we waiting for?" cried Grandma.

She switched on the engine and gripped the wheel.

BUT WAIT! The fog!

"My glasses," said Grandma. "My glasses!" She couldn't see with them and she certainly couldn't see without them. "What am I going to do?"

"Don't worry," said Billy. "I'll be your eyes for you. I can see through anything."

clang!
Clang!

So Grandma adjusted her cap and pushed the throttle. The lobsterboat churned through the waves.

""The buoy! The buoy!" cried Billy. "Hard to port! To port!"

Grandma swerved to the left—
just in the nick of time.

Clang! Clang!

The boat barreled past the point.

"The rocks! The rocks!" yelled Billy.
"Hard to starboard! To starboard!"

Grandma veered to the right—
without a moment to spare.

The boat sped toward the mainland.

-AWWRK! AWWRK!

"The dock! The dock!" shouted Billy. "Dead ahead! DEAD AHEAD!"

And Grandma cut the engine—just as the fog lifted from the shore.

"They're here! They're here!" everyone cheered.

Roy Hardy caught the rope and made it fast.
Edna Fillmore helped Billy, Burt, and Buster carry the lobsters.
And little Maggie Wells gave poor Bill a hand.

"All we need to do now is boil up some water," said Grandma.

Finally, the lobsters were ready. Grandma grabbed the tongs and leaned over the steaming pot. Then she laughed. "Oh, it's happened again," she said. "I can't see. Billy, be my eyes for me one more time!"

So, Billy stood beside Grandma until every single person's plate was piled high with food.

"Now, last but not least," said Grandma.
"This one's for you."

It was the biggest lobster Billy had ever seen.
And it was the tastiest, too!